HI! FLY GUY

Tedd Arnold

CARTWHEEL BOOKS
An Imprint of Scholastic Inc.

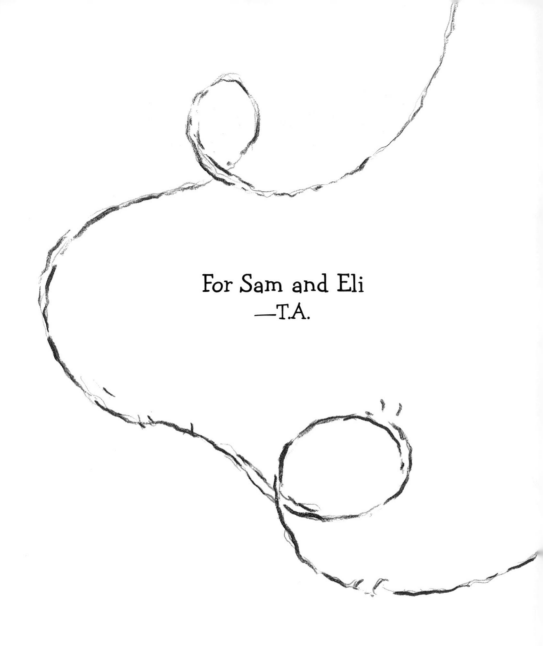

For Sam and Eli
—T.A.

ISBN 978-0-439-79914-0

Copyright © 2005 by Tedd Arnold. All rights reserved. Published by Scholastic Inc. SCHOLASTIC, CARTWHEEL BOOKS, and associated logos are trademarks and/or registered trademarks of Scholastic Inc.

24 23 22 21   20 21 22 23 24/0

Printed in the U.S.A.   40

First Scholastic paperback printing, September 2013

Chapter 1

A fly went flying.

He was looking
for something to eat—

something tasty,

something slimy.

A boy went walking.

He was looking for
something to catch—
something smart,
something for
The Amazing Pet Show.

They met.

BOINK

The boy caught the
fly in a jar.
"A pet!" he said.

The fly was mad.
He wanted to be free.
He stomped his foot
and said— BUZZ!

The boy was surprised.
He said, "You know my name!
You are the smartest pet in
the world!"

Chapter 2

Buzz took the fly home.

"This is my pet," Buzz said
to Mom and Dad.

"He is smart. He can say my name. Listen!"

Buzz opened the jar.
The fly flew out.

"Flies can't be pets!" said
Dad. "They are pests!"
He got the fly swatter.
The fly cried— BUZZ!

And Buzz came to the rescue.
"You are right," said Dad.
"This fly _is_ smart!"

"He needs a name," said Mom.
Buzz thought for a minute.
"Fly Guy," said Buzz.
And Fly Guy said—

BUZZ!

It was time for lunch.
Buzz gave Fly Guy
something to eat.

Fly Guy was happy.

Chapter 3

Buzz took Fly Guy to
The Amazing Pet Show.

The judges laughed.
"Flies can't be pets," they said.
"Flies are pests!"

Buzz was sad.
He opened the jar.
"Shoo, Fly Guy," he said.
"Flies can't be pets."

But Fly Guy liked Buzz.
He had an idea.
He did some fancy flying.

The judges were amazed.
"The fly can do tricks," they said.
"But flies can't be pets."

Then Fly Guy said—

The judges were more amazed. "The fly knows the boy's name," they said. "But flies can't be pets."

Fly Guy flew high, high, high
into the sky!

Then he dived down, down,
down into the jar.

"The fly knows his jar!" the judges said. "This fly <u>is</u> a pet!" They let Fly Guy in the show.

He even won an award.

And *so* began a beautiful
friendship.